HARRIS COUNTY PUBLIC LIBRARY

J Mic'...
Micha...
Texa... W9-ALN-943

$16.95
ocm57594032
06/23/2008

TEXAS
State Bird Pageant

Written by *Todd Michael*

Illustrated by *Lee Brandt Randall*

 QUAIL RIDGE PRESS

Copyright ©2005 by Todd Michael

All Rights Reserved.

No part of this book may be reproduced or transmitted in any form or by any means, electronic or mechanical, including photocopying, recording, or by any information storage and retrieval system, without permission in writing from the publisher.

Printed and bound in South Korea by Pacifica Communications.

9 8 7 6 5 4 3 2 1

QUAIL RIDGE PRESS

P. O. Box 123 • Brandon, MS 39043 • 1-800-343-1583
www.quailridge.com

Library of Congress Cataloging-in-Publication Data

Michael, Todd, 1968-
    Texas State Bird Pageant / by Todd Michael ; illustrated by: Lee Brandt Randall.
        p. cm.
    Summary: When Molly Mockingbird enters the Texas State Bird Beauty
Contest, she is ridiculed by the other contestants for being a copy
bird, until she finds her own true voice just in time.
    ISBN-13: 978-1-893062-75-7
    ISBN-10: 1-893062-75-9
        [1. Mockingbirds–Fiction. 2. Beauty contests–Fiction. 3. Songs–Fiction. 4. Texas–
Fiction.] I. Randall, Lee Brandt, 1955-, ill. II. Title.

PZ7 .M579827Tex 2005
[FIC]-dc22   2005002827

To bird lovers, bird-watchers,
and proud Texans
—Todd Michael

To David, for his amazing patience
—Lee Brandt Randall

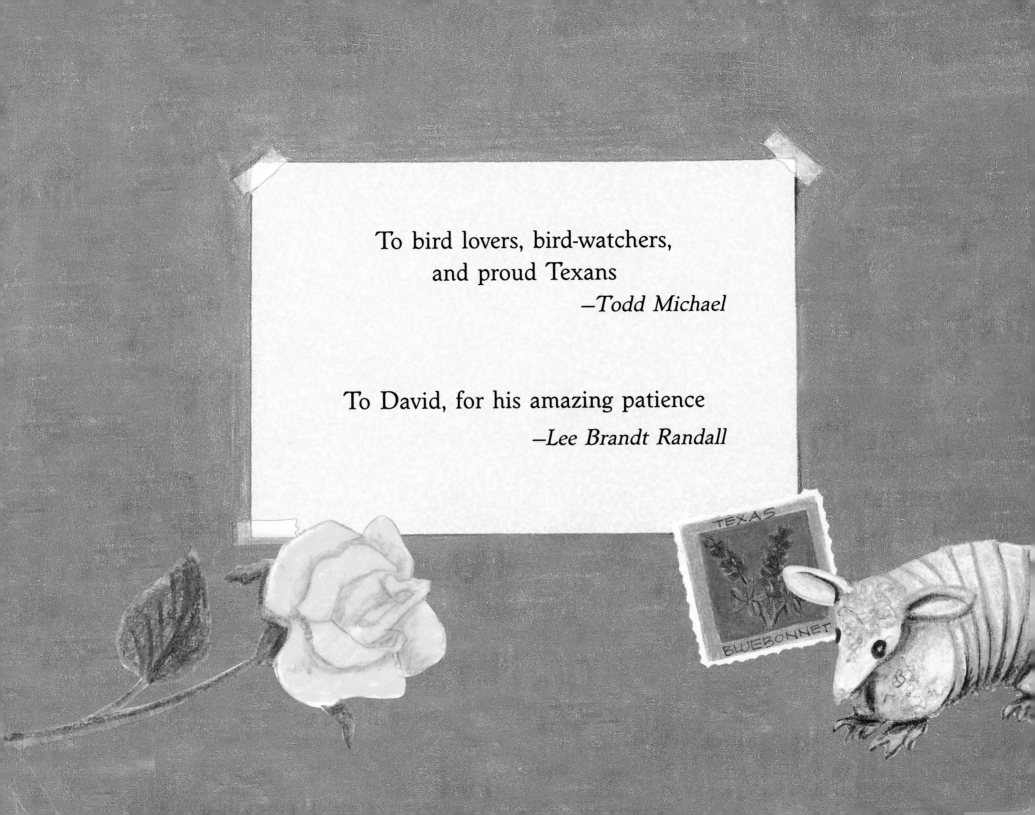

Deep in the heart of Texas, there lived a mockingbird named Molly.

Each morning at sunrise, she would listen to the unique songs of the other songbirds.
She often wished for a song of her very own to sing.

It was a rainy day in April when Molly first heard the news...
A beauty pageant was to be held in Austin.
All feathered females born in the Lone Star State were invited to take part in the event.
The prize was the title of Miss Texas State Bird.

Birds flew in from all over to get their names on that list!

Calling all 254 Counties

Texas
State Bird Beauty Pageant

Oh it's almost here!

It's a bird bonanza, extravaganza
And the day is getting near!
Seeking contestants in all shapes and sizes,
And we don't have lots of time!
Brighten your future, win fabulous prizes!
What a chance to shine!
It's a rare and splendid opportunity,
Coming soon to our community,
That day is getting near!
— The Texas State Bird Beauty Pageant,
Oh it's almost here!

P.S. No Horseflies Please!

VISIT BEAUTIFUL DOWNTOWN

AUSTIN, Texas

AUSTIN Welcomes You!

Many birds were signing up for the pageant. Reesie Robin flew in from Lubbock. Harriet Hawk came from Fort Worth. Quanah Quail arrived from Quitman. Rochelle Roadrunner ran all the way from Fort Bliss. Even Willa Warbler of Tyler showed up.

Tall birds and small birds, birds from Dallas and Beaumont, birds from Victoria and San Marcos, birds from Waco, Conroe, Bountiful, Fredericksburg, Midland, Laredo, Nacogdoches, Odessa, Brownsville, Brenham, Garland, Texarkana, Denton, Happy, Huntsville, Fort Stockton and Abilene.

As she looked around at all the birds gathered, Molly almost chickened out, but managed to get her name on the list just in time.

The following Saturday Molly went to the annual Seed and Insect Barbecue in Lockhart, and that is where the teasing and mean jokes began.

"You're not really going to be a contestant, are you?" asked Carley Cardinal of Plano.

For the Birds
Annual
SEED AND INSECT BBQ
Please join us for
Delicious cooking.
Delightful beverages
and
Dynam...

HELLO MY NAME IS
Molly

"I guess you'll sing another borrowed song for the talent competition," smirked Fanny Flycatcher of The Woodlands.

"Molly the Mimic, you are such a copy-bird," added Waxahachie native Paulette Egret.

Just then Erin Heron of Texas City shouted,
"Hey girls, listen to this one!"

The mockingbird, the mockingbird,
I guess by now you might have heard,
She'll steal your song, and mock each word,
The mockingbird, the mockingbird.

The birds chirped loudly,
as they repeated the silly rhyme,

The mockingbird, the mockingbird,
I guess by now you might have heard,
She'll steal your song, and mock each word,
The mockingbird, the mockingbird.

They laughed until Molly began to cry
and then finally fled for home.

The next morning Molly flew to Kingsville to visit her dear friend Gabby Green Jay.
"I could really use her good advice," thought Molly, as she approached Gabby's cozy birdhouse.
When Gabby saw Molly, she knew something was troubling her.
"You don't seem like yourself today. What's wrong?" questioned Gabby.
"It's the State Bird Beauty Pageant," answered Molly, as she began to cry again.
"The others tease me because I don't have a song of my own.
They call me things like Molly the Mimic, and they say I am not talented or original."
"I see," said Gabby, "but I think that's just a bunch of hogwash!"

Then Gabby started to play her piano and she sang this song to Molly...

You will find your own true voice.
They chirp and they chatter but that doesn't matter,
Just sing out loud and rejoice!
This dream that you seek, is a dream so unique,
I trust you'll make the right choice.
There's a song deep inside you, waiting to guide you,
You will find your own true voice! So go find your own true voice!

"I will try," promised Molly, as she began to leave. "Gabby, you always know how to lift my spirits."

A month flew by, and soon the big day was one week away.
Most of the contestants were busy rehearsing.

Isabella Spoonbill of Port Aransas was showing off her cheerleading skills.

Hailey Hummingbird of Wichita Falls read her acceptance speech to any creature who could stay awake long enough to hear the whole thing.

And Galveston's very own Lily Loon declared that she could NOT lose with her flapper-snapper dance routine!

Molly was both nervous and excited knowing the pageant was so close at wing. She had already started to work on an original song for the talent competition.

It was a song about the great state of Texas; she hoped to capture the pride she had always felt for her home state. She knew that if she wrote the lyrics, Gabby would gladly put music to her words.

For the next few days, the others continued to make fun of her. Still, she kept writing and exercising her vocal cords.

At last the day of the pageant had arrived! Molly had never seen so many birds in one place. Everybirdy was there to see who would be crowned Miss Texas State Bird.

When the others saw her, they began to snicker and bicker. Lucille Whippoorwill of Corpus Christi started it. "Molly, my dear, you might as well mosey on home right now. I intend to win this pageant. Just wait until you hear me sing 'Yellow Rose of Texas.'"

Guadeloupe Gull, a resident of Padre Island, joined in, "A bird without an original song wants to be our state bird? Now THAT'S funny!"

Then Owlma Owl of Amarillo said,
"WHO does she think she is? WHO would want a mockingbird
to represent this wonderful state? WHO?"

Texas State Bird
CONTESTANT #6

Molly Mockingbird
Austin

Gabby Green Jay had just arrived and she had overheard their unkind words. "For crying out loud! What are you girls doing?" asked Gabby. "Why must y'all hurt her feelings?"

"We were just pra-pra-practicing," Guadeloupe Gull said in a shaky, dishonest voice.

"That's not true," said Gabby. "I heard what was said, and every one of you should be ashamed!"

Soon they all scattered, leaving Molly and Gabby alone.

"How can I go through with this?" asked Molly.
"One minute I'm sure of myself and my song, then the next minute I'm scared."

"Don't you see?" asked Gabby. "They behave that way because
they are jealous of your sweet nature and your talent.
You have a gift for singing
their songs, even better
than they can sing
them. You also have
intelligence and
personality.

Molly, you're the most unselfish and kind bird I know.
Remember the time you brought me worm noodle soup when I was sick?
What's on the inside is much more important, not just talent or the way you look."

"So are you going to just stand there feeling sorry for yourself, or will you get out there and sing that precious song we both worked so hard on? The eyes of Texas are upon you!

It's like I said before...
You will find your own true voice!"

Molly listened carefully. She knew that Gabby was right.
She had come too far! There was simply no turning back now.

Suddenly a voice from the stage announced that it was time for the talent competition.

Bonita Blackbird of El Paso performed with a mariachi band.

Briana Bluebird of Houston did a
Texas-swing version of "Waltz Across Texas."
It was lively, to say the least!

And Miss Dovey Crockett of San Antonio
read some cowgirl poetry about the Alamo.

The pageant was only three hours long, but to Molly it seemed like forever.
She was surprised by her own courage when her turn came.
Gabby Green Jay played piano as Molly Mockingbird sang her original song...

Texas Pride: What I Love About Texas
by Molly McKenna Mockingbird

She's such a grand lady. The grandest I've seen...
She's longhorns and sagebrush and Tex-Mex cuisine.
She's canyons and deserts and bountiful grain,
She's a stroll through the prairie after the rain.
With farms and ranches where yellow roses grow,
She's a quick two-step. She's a waltz nice and slow.
Cowboys and oil fields and bowls of hot chili,
A place in your soul and so much more really!
She's tumbleweed, campfires, and ten-gallon hats,
She's saddles and spurs, Hill Country and bats.
She's mesquite and pecans and old wagon wheels,
She's soft like the blessing we say before meals.
Mesas and beaches, haciendas and lakes,
She's strong yet she's gentle. She's got what it takes!
She's there in the plains, and in every church bell,
She wears a bluebonnet; I know her so well...
She's an unspoken truth, you feel deep inside,

"Texas, Our Texas," my home and my PRIDE!

The audience loved it, and their applause was as loud as thunder. Gabby gave her a big hug as soon as they left the stage and said, "I knew you could do it!"

After the final contestant finished, the announcer asked, "Ladies and gentlebirds, who do you think will be our state bird?" Molly took a deep breath.

The announcer continued,
"We have some lovely and talented
ladies with us here today.

Yet, we can only have one winner.
This is the moment we have
all waited for.
Judges, the envelope please."

There was complete silence as he
opened it. Then he spoke...

"Let's put our wings together for
our official state bird,

Miss Molly Mockingbird!"

The other birds were upset; some pouted and stomped; others shrieked and shrilled.
But in their hearts, they knew that Molly Mockingbird was the best choice; for even though
they had treated her so badly, Molly just smiled and forgave them all.

As they placed the tiara on her head, Molly finally understood Gabby's words...
"You will find your own true voice."

Molly had found her true voice at last.
But really it had been there all the while!

And now you know how the mockingbird—
Molly Mockingbird, that is—
became the state bird of Texas!

The End

Some Interesting Facts about the Mockingbird:

- The mockingbird actually does possess a melodious song of its own.

- The mockingbird is a fierce protector of its nest.

- Like many songbirds, mockingbirds thrive on fruits and nuts.

- A mockingbird can mimic sounds such as that of a cackling hen, a barking dog and even notes from a piano.

- The mockingbird grows to about ten inches in length, including its tail.

- The mockingbird's nest can be found one to fifty feet above the ground, on the branch of a bush or in the fork of a tree.

- Mockingbirds can often be seen swooping down on a dog, cat or predator that may be venturing too close to its protected territory.

- The mockingbird was adopted as the state bird of Texas in 1927.

If you'd like to read more about mockingbirds, like Molly, visit your local library.

FRIENDSHIP

Other Texas State Symbols:

State Tree – Pecan
State Insect – Monarch Butterfly
State Flower – Bluebonnet
State Song – "Texas, Our Texas"
State Motto – the word "Friendship"

PECANS

TEXAS

BLUEBONNET

Listing of State Birds (Alphabetical by State):

Alabama – Yellowhammer

Alaska – Willow Ptarmigan

Arizona – Cactus Wren

Arkansas – Mockingbird

California – California Quail

Colorado – Lark Bunting

Connecticut – American Robin

Delaware – Blue Hen Chicken

District of Columbia – Wood Thrush

Florida – Mockingbird

Georgia – Brown Thrasher

Hawaii – Nene (a.k.a. Hawaiian Goose)

Idaho – Mountain Bluebird

Illinois – Cardinal

Indiana – Cardinal

Iowa – American Goldfinch

Kansas – Western Meadowlark

Kentucky – Cardinal

Louisiana – Brown Pelican

Maine – Black-Capped Chickadee

Maryland – Baltimore Oriole

Massachusetts – Black-Capped Chickadee

Michigan – American Robin

Minnesota – Common Loon

Mississippi – Mockingbird

Missouri – Eastern Bluebird

Montana – Western Meadowlark

Nebraska – Western Meadowlark

Nevada – Mountain Bluebird

New Hampshire – Purple Finch

New Jersey – American Goldfinch

New Mexico – Roadrunner

New York – Eastern Bluebird

North Carolina – Cardinal

North Dakota – Western Meadowlark

Ohio – Cardinal

Oklahoma – Scissor-Tailed Flycatcher

Oregon – Western Meadowlark

Pennsylvania – Ruffed Grouse

Rhode Island – Rhode Island Red (a.k.a. Chicken)

South Carolina – Carolina Wren

South Dakota – Ring-Necked Pheasant (a.k.a. Common Pheasant)

Tennessee – Mockingbird

Texas – Mockingbird

Utah – California Gull

Vermont – Hermit Thrush

Virginia – Cardinal

Washington – American Goldfinch

West Virginia – Cardinal

Wisconsin – American Robin

Wyoming – Western Meadowlark

A Special Note about the Green Jay of Texas:

Green Jays, like Gabby, are found in the lower Rio Grande Valley of Texas and no place else in the entire United States!

About the Author

Children's writer Todd Michael has lived in Dallas, Texas; Kansas City, Missouri; Destin, Florida; and New Orleans, Louisiana. Todd Michael attended elementary school in Tarkington Prairie, Texas, which is in Liberty County. He now calls Austin home. He is also the author of the children's book, *A Woolly Mammoth on Amelia Street*, a cookbook, *Jambalaya, Crawfish Pie, Filé Gumbo* and *The Louisiana State Bird Beauty Pageant* (under the pen name Todd-Michael St. Pierre). Todd Michael is a member of the Society of Children's Book Writers & Illustrators. You may read more about him and his books on his website at www.toddles.us.

About the Illustrator

Having grown up an Air Force brat, Lee Brandt Randall has called many places home, including Eagle Pass, in Maverick County, Texas. She currently lives with her husband and her daughter (and her dog, Mr. Bingley) in Baton Rouge, Louisiana, where she teaches art to middle school students.

© RANDY THOMAS

© AMY MONETT